I0456936

She's Gonna Get It Now!

She's Just Bad, Volume 1

Lucy Lafferty

Published by Lynda French, 2024.

This is a work of fiction. Similarities to real people, places, or events are entirely coincidental.

SHE'S GONNA GET IT NOW!

First edition. October 28, 2024.

Copyright © 2024 Lucy Lafferty.

ISBN: 978-1998074464

Written by Lucy Lafferty.

Table of Contents

In Lieu of Cash 1

The Firm Hand of the Law 7

A Painful How-To Lesson 14

Smutty Girl Talk 19

Premarital Domestic Discipline 24

Beta Has To Train His Alpha's Fated Mate 37

Sent To The Headmaster For a Hard Lesson 42

That String Bikini 54

Warden Gives Inmate a Parting Gift 61

The Honeymoon is Over 72

To naughty brats everywhere: you know you've been asking for it... now you're gonna get it!

About This Book

The bare bottoms of devious girls blush bright red when they're given well-deserved spankings. Such shame and humiliation at being disciplined - sometimes publicly - like a naughty child.

These ten stories range from punishment for bad behavior, learning what a spanking entails, an introduction to domestic discipline, sexual fantasies, and power plays that leave sorry girls desperately rubbing their sore behinds!

Enjoy reading about their plight knowing that the damage inflicted is never permanent and their physical discomfort doesn't last *too* long.

In Lieu of Cash

May arrives at the garage a few minutes ahead of her scheduled meeting with Roy Burton, the owner. She's puzzled by the smirk she sees on the face of Lenny, Roy's head mechanic. The man doesn't explain he just indicates that she should head into the boss's office.

The clicking of her high-heels rings loudly on the cement floor but the hallway leading into the back rooms is covered with indoor-outdoor carpet so May's approach is muffled, despite the office door being ajar.

The reason for Lenny's secretive smile is immediately apparent when May sees a young woman straddling Roy as he sits in his chair facing the doorway. The girl's tight skirt is hiked up over her thighs showing an expanse of bare leg while her blouse hangs down off her shoulders, evidently fully unbuttoned and open.

May's gasp of "Oh!" has the girl turning around and the older woman's shocked face is mirrored in the girl's look of surprise. Surprise turning into worry when they recognize each other. The girl in question is Bonnie, the daughter of May's fiancé Rick Dorrance who just happens to be Roy's best friend.

Bonnie struggles to stand up but Roy holds her in place. "I knew you'd be right on time May so I let this naughty girl keep trying it on with me so you could be a witness of what she's tryin' to do," he drawls.

Looking at Bonnie he adds: "Your daddy thinks the sun shines out of your delectable little ass and I don't want to be the one to tell him different. Now I'm sure that May here, seeing as she's the school headmistress, will knows just how to deal with bratty little girls like you. What do you think of this behavior, Principal Carson?"

May Carson slowly shakes her head at the sight of Bonnie Dorrance with her fully developed breasts straining against a sheer bra and the pink of her matching panties showing between her spread legs. The girl has climbed onto Roy Burton's lap and wrapped her arms around his neck while thrusting her nearly naked breasts in his face.

From the moment May began dating Rick his daughter went out of her way to be as rude and obstructive as possible. May has put up with a lot of nonsense from the teenager but now the shoe is on the other foot!

"I think Bonnie has some explaining to do. So go ahead young lady, and tell me why you're crawling half-naked all over your Dad's best friend?"

"I don't owe you an explanation, May! You're not my mother and you never will be even if you are going to marry my Dad. And talking about Dad why are you here? He said you have an appointment. Why are you seeing Dad's best friend behind his back, hmm?" The sassy miss is defiant as she challenges May.

"I'm happy to tell you what Roy and I are doing, even though I'm not sure you deserve an explanation... However, I'm here because we're finalizing our plans for your father's surprise birthday party tomorrow night. Obviously we can't meet when your Dad is around because it's a surprise, and you don't know anything about it because, again, it's a surprise and we don't trust you.

Now it's your turn to explain why you've stripped down and climbed onto Roy like a slutty lap dancer."

"I'm not! But... Roy did my oil change and.. and I don't have the money to pay him so I thought maybe he'd take a bit of fooling around as payment. I mean, it's only a bit of fun."

"But Bonnie your father gave you the money to pay Roy, I know because I was there and I saw him do so. In fact he gave you extra even though we all know there's no chance you'd ever return the change."

"Well yeah, but I had some shopping to do and—"

"And you thought you'd flash your tits at an old guy, maybe even let him have a squeeze, and he'd be happy to write off your bill, eh? You probably figured you could blackmail me into extra freebies in future.

You know, I'm not all that old Bonnie, and I can still pick up chicks of my own type which is grown women not bratty teenagers flaunting themselves."

The girl's face blushes bright red with angry embarrassment at being shamed like a child. An identical idea strikes both of the adults who exchange a look and wry smiles of understanding.

Lifting Bonnie as he stands up Roy places her face-down on his desk suggesting: "A naughty brat should be soundly spanked and May, between the two of us I think we can deliver the proper spanking this girl deserves."

"I completely agree, Roy," replies May as she tugs Bonnie's skirt up over her hips to her waist. "A good old-fashioned spanking on her bare bottom."

"NO! Don't you dare!" hollers a shocked Bonnie.

Roy reaches over and pulls the flimsy panties right down. "There that's good," he says, "From this position we can see the tits she was so anxious to show off and her pretty ass all exposed and just begging to be punished. She's gonna get it now!"

He leans closer and starts smacking Bonnie's plump bottom as she squirms and squeals. After delivering a half-dozen or so slaps he steps back and gestures to May to continue.

"No, you can't! Don't touch me!" cries the girl in outraged humiliation. She can't believe her father's girlfriend is seeing this - doing this!

May applies brisk, stinging slaps over the same area Roy has already paddled. "I'm acting *in loco parentis*, Bonnie, and you will accept this punishment without complaint or else we'll have tell your Dad what you've done."

"No, don't tell him please!" begs Bonnie. She doesn't want to lose her father's good opinion of herself, he's always spoiled her and treated her like his little princess.

"We won't if you promise to never try something like this ever again," says Roy taking another turn to work on the naughty girl's rapidly reddening backside.

"And you will re-pay Roy for the work he's done using cash this time, right?"

"Yes! Yes, I will now please stop, it really hurts," pleads Bonnie her expression contrite and tears spilling from her eyes.

"Oh I'm quite sure you've got a long ways to go yet!" snickers May, "But I'll stop so I can step back and enjoy this great show you're putting on. You really know how to wiggle those hips and set your fat little bottom jiggling for Roy, young lady.

And Roy, you have hidden talents! I never knew you were an expert spanker. You've got Bonnie dancing with every smack so I bet it really stings! Please continue with the lesson."

"Yeah Boss, continue," says Lenny lounging in the doorway. Bonnie shrieks *go away!* hating to have her nakedness exposed like this in front of the old garage-hand but neither May nor Roy tell him to leave so he gets an eyeful. *It's a real pleasure to see this sassy little madam getting exactly what she deserves,* he thinks with satisfaction.

Happy to show off his expertise Roy spanks all over Bonnie's bottom including the tops of her thighs. She's soon sobbing, in shame and pain, but he doesn't let up landing stroke after stroke until her pleas become incoherent cries of *I won't... please no...* and *no more!*

She's wailed so loudly she hasn't noticed that a couple of the part-time crew have arrived at the office to see what all the noise is about. These boys go to the same school as Bonnie and from the evidence of their happy grins it's clear she's well-known to them.

"Look at the stuck-up bitch getting her ass tanned!" exclaims one school-mate while the other chimes in to agree that it's *fucking great to see the little cocktease being taught a lesson!*

Bonnie's head whips round at the sound of their voices and with her face blushing as red as her bottom she squeezes her eyes shut in utter humiliation.

"I'd offer you boys a go but this isn't playtime, it's punishment. If you want to enjoy giving a sexy spanking to Bonnie you'll just have to make a date—"

"Never!" screams Bonnie enraged.

Roy just chuckles until one of the guys pulls out his phone then he says: "Uh-uh, no videos. But you boys have the evidence of your own eyes so I suggest you could practise a little blackmail to get her co-operation.

If you two promise to keep your mouths shut at school I bet you can persuade this little minx to show her appreciation for your continued silence."

The teenagers can't contain the grins that light their faces at the thought of having a hold over Bonnie Dorrance!

Relentlessly, Roy keeps spanking Bonnie's hot red bottom until she's begging for mercy. He shoos away the audience although Bonnie is well past the point of caring who sees what so long as the punishment just stops.

Afterwards she just lies across the desk limply. It's May who hoists up the girl's panties and pulls down her skirt admonishing her to behave properly in future.

"If you ever act up like that again you'll find yourself across your Daddy's knee and his spanking will be extra painful because he'll be so disappointed in you."

"I won't! I promise! Please, please don't tell Daddy," Bonnie pleads, her tear-streaked face showing sincere remorse.

Roy turns the girl towards him and after manhandling her breasts he pulls her blouse closed and warns her that she's got a month to come up with his money... *or else!*

Bonnie's hands fly to cover her sore backside as she nods frantically, hiccuping back her sobs and desperately anxious to avoid ever feeling Roy's wrath unleashed on her tender bottom again.

The End

The Firm Hand of the Law

Officer Jensen shakes his head in dismay. Both the drunk driver of this car and his passenger are lucky that the collision wasn't much worse. Fortunately, no one is injured but the young man will be spending the night in jail and the young lady will need a lift home.

Looking at her ID Jack Jensen recognizes the address and also her surname. "Are you Sgt. William Millican's daughter?" he asks.

The pouting girl gives a tearful nod and Jensen realizes she's missing her Daddy's comfort right now.

"I'll see you safely home," glancing at her name he adds, "Stephanie. Come with me."

Leaving the booking of the hapless drunken boy to his partner and the back-up team, Jensen leads the girl to the police cruiser to drive her home.

Stephanie and her date had almost reached her place when the accident occurred so the trip doesn't take long. Seeing a police car pull into the driveway brings Audrey Millican running out the door, her hands clasped tightly together.

Recognizing the fearful look of dread on her face Jack Jensen is quick to call out: "Everything's okay, Audrey. Stephanie was in a car crash but she isn't hurt and I've brought her home."

"Is that you Jack? Jack Jensen? Oh thank God. I don't know what I thought when I saw the police car..."

"For chrissake's Ma, give it a rest willya?" slurs Stephanie.

Audrey bites down on her bottom lip while Jack's mouth purses in annoyance. "That's no way to speak to your mother, young lady," he admonishes before nodding at Audrey to head back inside.

Nothing further is said while the three of them get indoors and the front door is closed. Then Jack turns to the errant girl insisting she apologize for her language and tone.

Stephanie squints up at him, her face in a scowl, before saying: "Fuck you, mister cop."

Quick as a flash Jack seats himself on a wooden bench in the foyer and pulls the girl across his knee, dragging down her leggings and thong. Audrey watches in shock as he delivers a series of heavy-handed stinging smacks to the her teenage daughter's bare bottom.

Audrey begins protesting: "Oh! I don't think..." but her words trail off as Stephanie spews a stream of shocking profanity.

Jack Jensen simply doubles his efforts and Audrey's lips form a tiny smile of satisfaction as Stephanie's swearing turns to pleas and promises, while her backside turns a painful shade of red.

Now when the officer demands an apology to her mother Stephanie quickly cries: "I'm sorry, Mommy!"

Lifting the girl back onto her feet Jack Jensen looks into her tear-streaked face with the warning that he'll be back at the ten in the morning in order to finish, with suitable reinforcement, tonight's lesson before going in to work for his 11-to-7 shift.

Stephanie wails: "MOM!" and Audrey does frown with uncertainty until Jack explains that tonight's spanking was for Stephanie's disrespect. Tomorrow's punishment will be for the much more serious infraction of underage drinking and getting into a car with a drunk driver.

"You're old enough to know better than to indulge in such reckless behavior, Stephanie. What if you'd ended up in hospital or worse, at the morgue? How would your father feel being stationed halfway around the world, fighting for his country, while you're breaking your mother's heart here at home?"

The girl's sobs don't take the stern look off his face.

"I've seen too much in my career to treat this sort of thing lightly, young lady. You will be thoroughly spanked again tomorrow morning and that's all there is to it."

Nodding to the girl's mother he lets himself out of their house and drives off.

Stephanie throws herself into her mother's arms begging for her protection from *that nasty old cop.* Audrey makes soothing noises while wondering what she should do.

After settling her daughter in bed Audrey heads into her own room wondering what her husband will say when he learns what's happened. Although it's been years Audrey still recalls the several occasions she found herself upended across his knee while he expressed his displeasure with his wife by administering a sound spanking.

She's anxious and still undecided about what to do next morning when Officer Jensen arrives promptly at 10:00. He senses her hesitation and speaks firmly telling her to let him in.

Once inside he simply asks Audrey what she thinks her husband would do if he were home?

"Oh Jack, if Will wasn't away I don't Stephanie would be like this. He was supposed to be finished with the Army but they pressured him into signing up for another eighteen months and she took it hard. She's always been a Daddy's girl and I think she's acting out or something. As for me well you know how it is with teenage girls and their mothers... I can't do anything right."

"Audrey I do know exactly what you mean. I have two girls myself and though they're grown now when they were teens both of them were subjected to bare-bottomed sessions across my knee. Every time they got a spanking it happened under my wife's watchful eye and lasted until she was satisfied they'd learned their lesson.

You see, Margaret couldn't hit hard enough to get the message across and I'm sure you can't either, Audrey. I'm also positive Will would get the job done without hesitation."

"Yes, I think you're right but oh Jack it just feels... I don't know, somehow wrong? Or something? I mean even the schools aren't allowed to use corporal punishment any more."

"Actually I've always had mixed feelings about that. While I agree that discipline should happen immediately I also believe correction should come from a parent or at least in the presence of a parent. But, as you've pointed out, that's no longer an issue. The responsibility has been taken away from the schools.

Now Audrey, something has to be done about Stephanie's actions. Getting in a car with a drunk driver could have killed her but the strict letter of the law doesn't care about that. It does care about her underage drinking though.

If you don't want me to give Stephanie a spanking then of course I won't but in that case I'll have to take her to the station for booking. I'm sure you'll be able to pick her up right away because the judge will probably just give her a lecture so it's not going to ruin her life or anything but the decision is yours."

"And mine, I think," says Stephanie stepping into the hallway. The girl's head is hanging low but with a deep breath for courage she shows her pale, hungover face with its red-rimmed eyes. "I don't want to be spanked again but... I don't want to go to the police station so choosing between the two well, I uh... I guess the um, spanking."

"Oh honey are you sure about this? Because I'm pretty certain it's going to be worse than last night's punishment and that had you crying your eyes out."

"I'm sure, but I want to keep my pants on—"

Interrupting the girl Jack Jensen flatly states: "No way. Underage drinking is a criminal offence. The spanking serves a dual purpose acting as punishment for what you did and as a deterrent, a preventative measure, so you don't repeat your bad behavior. It's a punishment Stephanie and it's going to hurt enough to make you a very sorry girl with a very sore bottom."

When she says nothing further he takes her hand and leads her back to the same bench he used last night. Sitting down the policeman positions Stephanie across his knee and taking hold of her pyjama bottoms he pulls them down to her knees. She shivers under the combined scrutiny of the officer and her mother on her nakedness, feeling the thick fabric of his uniform pants against her bare thighs.

Jack tells Audrey: "I spoke to Margaret about this last night and she reminded me that when our girls reached their late teens I no longer spanked them by hand. Instead, I used a wooden-backed hairbrush, in fact this very one here," he reaches into his jacket pocket and pulls out a solid oval-shaped hairbrush.

"Margaret dug it out of the drawer thinking you might find this more appropriate than me using my hand on her."

11

"Oh yes! I think that's best, please thank Margaret for me," Audrey gratefully exclaims, having no idea that such an implement will deliver a much more painful punishment.

Stephanie has been thinking about how shameful it is to be lying on Officer Jensen's lap fully exposed like this instead of listening to their conversation. It's a shock to hear the *CRACK!* of the hairbrush just moments before a hot, thudding pain floods her right cheek.

She's in mid-yelp when the second *CRACK!* comes down on the left side. And so her terrible ordeal continues with the rat-a-tat sound of the smacks steadily applied to her wiggling bottom.

"Oh no, no! *CRACK!* Stop! *CRACK!* I changed my mind... *CRACK!* I don't want this! *CRACK!*" The girl keeps crying out her protests while writhing across the officer's lap in an effort to escape that punishing hairbrush. Jack Jensen keeps a firm hold on the squirming teen and his appraising eye determines she can take plenty more swats.

He catches himself smiling at the very satisfactory sound of each painful smack, both the *CRACK!* and the squeal, a memory he'd forgotten ever since his girls married and moved to homes of their own.

Stephanie's *oohs* and *ows* get louder and louder the longer her punishment continues. Soon she's kicking her legs while trying to reach her hands back to cover her burning flesh. Jack efficiently puts a stop to that by trapping her legs under one of his own and capturing both wrists to pin beneath her.

Now that he's got her held firmly in place he's able to resume the firm paddling. Jack is determined to give Miss Stephanie Millican a lesson she won't soon forget. The girl is wailing and sobbing by time her bottom is blisteringly hot and colored a bright red all over.

When Jack releases her she runs to stand behind her mother, bouncing up and down rubbing her tender rear while howling like a child.

Jack returns the innocent-looking hairbrush, a very effective implement, to his pocket and tells Audrey that if Stephanie shows any signs of backsliding into naughty behavior she just has to pick up the phone to schedule another session.

"Oh I don't think that's going to be necessary, right Stephanie?"

"No Mommy," sobs the girl sounding more like seven then her actual age of seventeen as she rubs her sore behind. "I'll never, ever, ever need another spanking!"

Saying *I'll be in touch* Jack Jensen gives Audrey Millican a wink that she returns with a knowing smile.

The End

A Painful How-To Lesson

Carrie is reassured by the man's professional manner but still apprehensive to be where she is and doing what she's doing. But the money is good - very, very good - and Jax promised no one will see her face.

Mr Stevens himself greets Carrie at the door of his office in this rundown building. It's 9:00 at night and his staff probably went home at the usual time. He compliments her on her punctuality as he invites her inside.

It isn't a big suite, just an anteroom with a secretary's desk and filing cabinets leading to a larger office with white walls suitable for filming the video. The camera set-up looks elaborate but the furnishings consist of only one piece, a raised bench that reminds Carrie of the *vaulting horse* from gym class.

Positioned in the middle of the room the spanking bench is well-lit by the overhead light which exposes signs of wear and tear on the padded vinyl top.

Mr Stevens helps Carrie to bend her body across the bench with her head hanging down over the side, hidden from the camera. Checking she is comfortable he then secures her wrists to the padded cuffs attached to the bench legs. That's unexpected, but he moves so quickly her binding is done before she can protest.

"I'm going to start now, my dear, and since there's audio with the video be aware that anything and everything you say will be recorded."

Carrie nods, determined not to utter a sound.

Mr Stevens clicks some buttons then begins by welcoming the viewing audience. He explains they are in for a special treat since this episode features a *Spanking Virgin* called Missy.

"I'll be demonstrating different techniques using various implements to ensure a proper punishment. You, the audience, and Missy will both learn the how-to basics of administering an old-fashioned, painful punishment spanking.

Carrie shifts a bit at his words before remembering that Jax said she'd mostly be acting for the camera.

Mr Stevens draws close to her and taking hold of the hem of the schoolgirl-uniform skirt she's been told to wear pulls it up to her waist, exposing her panty-clad bottom. She's also been told to wear full-coverage white panties.

Explaining himself to the camera Mr Stevens starts smacking her bottom. He has big strong hands and Carrie feels the sting of each swat. After a dozen or so strokes she can't control her twitching since her whole behind is now feeling sensitive.

All of a sudden Mr Stevens yanks her panties down to her knees. Although she knew this would happen she's still startled. He rubs her bare flesh and discusses how it's pinked up nicely despite her underwear providing some coverage.

Now he begins spanking in earnest and encourages his viewers to listen to the even cadence of his strokes and that very satisfying smacking sound of palm against flesh.

"I'll give Missy about five minutes by hand on the bare then once she's warmed up we'll explore the leather strap and possibly the wooden paddle."

He continues with increased vigor and soon Missy is emitting muffled cries as her flesh blooms from pink to rosy red. She squirms, twists, and wriggles but she can't escape that punishing hand.

"There now, that's a lovely color and," Mr Stevens lays his palm on her tender globes, "yes, burning hot. But we have quite a ways to go yet."

He says the words in a teasing tone but Carrie isn't fooled. She's heard how his breathing got harder and knows he's enjoying himself.

Still smartly spanking her stinging bottom Mr Stevens continues to educate his audience about tempo and rhythm, pacing and placement, but Carrie can't hear him over her rising panic at the growing pain in her backside. It's on fire!

She starts to buck and writhe and this response encourages more pedantry from Mr Stevens as he points out just how much she flinches and quivers and spasms.

Then he picks up the belt, doubles it in his fist, and starts slashing down against her blazing cheeks. Carrie howls but Mr Stevens keeps slapping her flesh with stroke after stroke.

Why did I ever let Jax talk me into this? It's horrible! it hurts so much! she thinks with desperate regret. Her earlier determination to keep quiet is completely forgotten as she yelps and hollers at the biting pain.

When Carrie kicks her legs her panties fall down from her knees and Mr Stevens snatches them away from her ankles. As her legs piston wildly his audience gets an eyeful of her most private parts.

"Now pay attention because this is the important bit," announces Mr Stevens. "Just when it seems like the naughty girl can't possibly take any more it's crucial that you push on even harder. Move on to another spanking tool, for Missy I'm choosing this wide wood-backed hairbrush, and really let fly."

He suits his action to his words and begins a rapid tattoo. Carrie shrieks and wails and cries out for him to please-please-please stop but Mr Stevens simply moves down to her tender sit spot and the soft skin of her upper thighs.

"The buttocks and thighs are fleshy areas which can take a lot of punishment. Personally, I like to think that this is God's deliberate design. Whichever higher power you believe in, or if you prefer: evolution, wayward girls have the prettiest bottoms and that makes our task easy and enjoyable."

He spanks again and again, up and down, left to right, each stroke heavy and hard until Carrie's whole body goes rigid for a moment before she collapses sobbing. Only then does he stop.

"Now we're there. You see it, right? You see how we pushed past the boundaries of wilful defiance into defeated surrender. This is a well-disciplined girl who won't be misbehaving anytime soon.

Are you wondering what exactly was her offence? Foolish spending that landed her in debt, a common enough infraction among young ladies, and one that well... I'm sure she'll commit again!" He pauses, once again admiring her glowing bottom before turning back to the camera with a smirk saying: "And we know what to do when that happens, hmm?

Thank you for subscribing to my channel, and please leave your comments below."

Mr Stevens clicks off the recording but stays to watch the *likes* accumulate and to read the comments. It isn't until Carrie groans that he remembers the girl still slumped over the spanking bench and crying piteously.

He dumps a squirt of cooling aloe on her burning flesh and absentmindedly smooths it in with his eyes still glued to his laptop.

Coming around he reaches down to uncuff her wrists telling her she's put on a terrific show. "You're a natural and the camera loves you! All these *likes* tell me you were really popular with the live audience and I'll bet this video racks up plenty of replays. I hope you'll come back for another session, Missy."

Standing Carrie pulls her skirt down and doesn't bother correcting him. She spies her panties and balls them up to go in her purse. Seeing her with her bag Mr Stevens takes out his wallet and slips out four crisp $50 bills. Taking another look at all the positive comments on his channel he adds a fifth $50 and urges her to think about returning.

Suffering such extreme pain in her backside she can't bear to thank him but she does nod acknowledging the payment and tip.

"I really appreciate the great job you did my dear, and I truly hope you'll get in touch to film another episode," Mr Stevens says guiding her out of his office.

Walking stiffly but as quickly as she's able Carrie heads for the elevator knowing she can't manage even the one flight of stairs down.

But she bites back any angry words because well... you never know when the allure of impulse shopping will make those bills pile up again.

The End

Smutty Girl Talk

"What's the secret fantasy you're most ashamed of enjoying?"

"Believe it or not... huh, this is pretty embarrassing for a feminist to admit to but it's um, getting a spanking."

"NO WAY! That's one of my favorites, too! C'mon, tell me how yours plays out."

"That's a coincidence, huh? Anyhow, for me it starts with a domineering man telling me I'm a naughty brat who needs to be taught a lesson. That if I don't apologize for my behavior *right now* he'll put me across his knee and give me a good old-fashioned spanking on my bare bottom."

"Oooh, bad girl! I want all the details."

"Okay. I'm with this gorgeous macho man—"

"Bill?"

"God no, not my boyfriend, my fantasy boyfriend. Who's something other than a boyfriend actually, I'm not clear on that part. Anyhow, I'm acting up and I know I'm pushing his buttons but I keep at it and watch him get more and more exasperated with me. Finally he makes the threat I just mentioned about a good old-fashioned spanking on my bare bottom and I stick out my tongue in reply."

"Of course you do."

"Well that's a game-changer. Suddenly he's no longer annoyed and frustrated with me, oh no, he's smiling. He's gone from pissed-off to *anticipating-with-pleasure* and I think *uh-oh, I'm in big trouble now.* And boy am I ever!

Next thing I know I'm face-down and bottom-up and no matter how hard I struggle to stop him he just holds me firmly and – this is the worst part – he laughs at me. He tells me I'm going to get exactly what I've been asking for, and he's going to enjoy every minute although I won't.

I'm braless in a simple halter dress that he pulls up and over my shoulders. He doesn't take it right off me, instead he leaves it bunched up with the fabric trapping my arms.

When he fingers the waistband of my panties – for some reason it's always panties, never a thong – I start begging and pleading with him not to take them down while promising to behave but he just yanks them to my knees. Being exposed like this, with my arms tangled in my dress and my panties wrapped around my knees, makes me feel even more naked then complete nudity.

Then it starts.

He gives me a sound spanking, alternating left to right and up and down, for a solid five minutes until he tells me I'm *a nice rosy red*.

The loud slapping sound of each swat, his happy chuckles as I flinch and squirm, the sting on my poor bum... there's a full-length mirror on the wall and he orders me to turn my head so I can see the entire side view of naked me across his lap and the full view of his face with its mean smile.

It's so humiliating to have to watch my body writhe and squirm as each smack makes me wiggle for his pleasure but... it's also like watching a movie of someone else getting their bare bottom properly punished and crazy as it sounds I envy that helpless girl because she looks so sexy and that really turns me on.

And he's talking the whole time. Telling me how delightful it is to punish my luscious ass, how every jiggle and every squeal is pure thrill, and he's going to enjoy stretching this into a really lengthy session. He gives me a running commentary on how my twitching just invites him to administer harder blows, how every flinch is an invitation for him to inflict more, and how I'm coloring up so nicely from pink to rose to a really deep pink and soon-to-be red.

Since begging didn't do me any good I try fighting: yelling and swearing and making all kinds of threats. He only increases the tempo and moves down to my sit spots and the tops of my thighs. He points out that the more I insult him the more obvious it becomes that *I haven't learned my lesson yet.*

So I try to be quiet but I can't help the gasps and whimpers that escape. Every inch of my bottom is burning hot and each new stroke lands on an already tender spot with a sharp sting. I know my hips are dancing wildly, trying to avoid his punishing hand but that's impossible.

Finally he stops and asks how humiliated I feel. I refuse to answer but then he slips his fingers between my legs and omigod I'd soaking. The wet sucking sound his rubbing fingers make truly does shame me. And the groan of pleasure when he sinks two fingers inside and hooks my g-spot is matched by little gasping cries that I can't control as his thumb circles my clit.

He tells me my humiliation is divine and exquisite and I completely shatter with a huge orgasm.

I don't get it. I hate being spanked, it hurts and makes me feel foolish, but at the same time my whole groin is flooded with heat. I'm ready to accept whatever he wants to do next except he comments that *obviously I've been craving a proper punishment from my firm-handed Master* and that makes me screech in anger.

So of course now he says that if I'm in denial it means I need more correction and he continues spanking me with harder strokes and at a faster pace until I'm bouncing and kicking my legs. It's so embarrassing to hear him say how much he enjoys the spectacle of me wriggling and writhing with every smack. He tells me my pretty ass is even prettier when it's painted red with his hand-prints, and blisteringly hot to the touch.

Then he thanks me for the entertainment! I'm being thoroughly disciplined and it's so, so shaming."

"And how does it end?"

"I don't know, I've already shattered by time I reach that point in the scenario."

"Oh damn. Okay, I'll tell you what I like to imagine, maybe you'll cum twice!

First off, my man is a real tough guy, a prick who terrifies me at the same time he makes me willing to crawl if it will please him. When he's going to spank me he tells me well in advance so I have plenty of time to anticipate both the pain and the pleasure.

My guy would say he won't stop spanking my bum until I beg to suck my Master's cock..."

"So naturally I resist until I'm sobbing with a fire-engine red behind..."

"Then I drop to my knees between his legs and he gets to enjoy seeing my face all red and teary while I gag and drool over his big dick..."

"And he uses one hand to hold my head in place and the other to pull my dress off so he can fondle my tits with the hot palm of his hand..."

"As he looks over my shoulder into the mirror to admire how red he's beat my ass..."

"That's when he tells me to suck him dry, swallowing every drop. Then I get on my hands and knees facing away from him but towards the mirror so I can watch myself as I masturbate until he gets hard again and can fuck me doggie-style."

"Damn, that's really hot."

"Fuck girl, we've made ourselves a great fantasy."

"What if..."

"No!"

"Ha-ha... *maybe!*"

The End

Premarital Domestic Discipline

Maggie casts another sidelong glance at Ken and once again he has to struggle to maintain the serious expression he's worn ever since Pastor Jonathan began speaking.

The two of them are in premarital training along with a few other couples, most their own age but one older pair, and the subject has taken an... *interesting* turn. Pastor Jonathan is explaining the meaning of *Domestic Discipline* within a good Christian marriage.

Ken is willing to accept the role as Head of Household but he's having trouble believing that Maggie will submit to being *taken in hand.* When Pastor Jonathan details exactly what he means by that well... Ken doesn't dare meet Maggie's gaze, there's no way she'll ever accept that!

At the murmuring from his audience the pastor pauses the lecture and gives them a reassuring smile.

"I know this is something new to all of you and it will take a bit of time to absorb but I can guarantee this is one of the most important ingredients in the recipe for a long, happy, and fulfilling marriage."

"Easy for you to say!" bursts out Maggie and everyone joins in to laugh. Even Pastor Jonathan chuckles for a moment before turning serious once again.

"Surprisingly enough it's not easy on the husband, Margaret. Of course the first time is the hardest but it's never a simple undertaking. There is always a lot of emotion involved. That's one of the reasons I counsel that you men never punish your wives if you're in a temper. Although I've told you that swift correction is preferred you cannot administer it unless you're in a calm frame of mind."

"Just wait til your Father gets home!" stage-whispers Maggie.

"Margaret, please. I want you to keep an open mind about this and listen to what my wife has to say on the matter."

With that Pastor Jonathan nods to his wife, Amelia, who comes forward from the back of the room to address the group face-to-face. Like him she is in her forties and despite a face scrubbed free of make-up the beauty she'd once been is still evident in her youthful good looks.

Smiling at all of us she begins by dropping a bombshell: "I don't like being spanked by my husband and neither do your mothers, but I can promise you each and every one of them has been disciplined by your fathers, and on more than one occasion."

Turning towards her husband her smile broadens when she adds: "None of us is as well-behaved as we ought to be."

Pastor Jonathan nods and gives his wife a wry grin. Amelia continues explaining:

"When Jonathan decides that my shortcomings add up to meriting punishment I always want to argue and justify my actions. He listens patiently and might even drop one or two items off the list of infractions if my reasoning is sound, but I am never able to convince him not to spank me. He never leaves that decision up to me because it's his job to shoulder that burden.

By accepting his duty to provide me with the proper care – whether by a soft hand if I need nursing or a hard hand if I need discipline – he provides me with the stability and security I need. I have placed my trust in my husband, knowing he will not fail to protect and guide me."

"But isn't it... well, abusive? If he beats you?" asks one of the brides-to-be.

"No, absolutely not, because it's not a beating, it's a spanking. We're not fighting, he's teaching me a lesson. Or, more likely, reinforcing a lesson I already learned but chose to ignore.

For example, the last time Jonathan punished me it was because I needed to get my snow tires put on but since that always means a long wait at the garage I kept putting it off until the snow actually fell and I ended up skidding into a ditch. I wasn't hurt but I could have been or I could have hurt someone else. I was in the wrong and knew it.

Even worse I was out of cellphone range so it was actually a policeman who came by and radioed to the station to make the call. Putting my life in danger is number one on the list of absolute worst things I can do so I knew I was in for a severe punishment."

Pastor Jonathan had moved to lean against his desk but now he stands up straight and takes the floor saying: "That phone call was..." he pauses to clear his throat, obviously reliving the emotion that the memory evoked.

"It was so frightening. Once I knew Amelia was safe I said a prayer of thanks, of course, but I also prayed that God would give me the strength to apply the spanking her risky behavior warranted. More importantly, I prayed for the mercy to keep my angry fear in check or else I'd be giving her the whipping of her life."

"Jonathan already knew that I was penitent and apologetic. His job was to make me regretful as well and he certainly accomplished that task. He has never used a whip on me, that was just a figure of speech, but I was subjected to the leather paddle, or the wooden paddle with the holes drilled in it, or his belt every day for a week. In addition to hard hand-spankings."

"But that's awful!" exclaims an indignant Maggie. "Your wife didn't want to end up in the ditch and if you really did care so much about her welfare you'd just be grateful she was safe instead of tormenting her like that, and for days too!"

Ken puts his hand on her arm but she is visibly upset. Amelia comes over and taking both of Maggie's hands in hers assures her that she never for a moment doubted she deserved every stroke. Her punishment was just and in fact she'd requested extra spankings for the fear and pain that she'd caused her husband through her own thoughtlessness.

"I'm sure he was perfectly happy to give you extra!"

"No, but only because it's never up to the wife when, how, or how long her punishment should be. Jonathan did give me extra corner time because he wanted me to understand that I needed to forgive myself."

"Corner time?" asks a puzzled Ken.

"I've heard mention of this *corner time* before," says the older man in the group. "Can you explain what it is?"

Pastor Jonathan takes over again lecturing that corner time is a necessary component of domestic discipline. It can occur before the spanking, in between spankings, or afterwards, or in any combination. It involves contemplation, humiliation, and finally acceptance of the rightness of the punishment.

The protocol he and Amelia follow is that she will go to the study, fetch whatever spanking implement he's chosen, close the drapes, remove all garments below her waist, and then get in position. That means bending over the low-backed sofa to wait for her spanking.

After it's been administered Jonathan will send his wife to stand in the corner with her hands on her head because rubbing her sore red bottom is strictly forbidden. He will question her and, depending on her answers, will then decide if she's been sufficiently punished or is in need of further correction.

If he deems that more is required he provides it. The final component, also a vital part of the proceedings, is the after-care. The husband will take his tearful wife in his arms to comfort her and confirm that he still loves her and she now has a clean slate.

"The feeling I get after Jonathan has done his loving duty by me is one of peace, acceptance, and thankfulness. I don't expect you to understand what I'm saying but I know, 100 percent, that you will come to know it for yourselves."

The pastor's wife speaks with such conviction that the engaged couples are exchanging glances and squeezing hands. Except Maggie. She is biting her lip to hold back her laughter.

At first she'd been angry but once she got a mental image of Ken telling her to go prepare for a punishment spanking – and herself meekly obeying! - she has to struggle to keep her face straight.

"I recommend each of you continue this discussion with each other and perhaps with your parents or an older married sibling as well. You'll probably have questions or concerns that they can address. And of course both Amelia and I are happy to offer counsel anytime it's required."

The meeting breaks up shortly afterwards and the couples file out. Looking back Maggie sees Pastor Jonathan's eyes on her. His expression is serious, but not annoyed or impatient. She feels that somehow she's fallen short in his estimation but that thought only makes her defiant.

Once she's safely buckled into Ken's pick-up Maggie lets her mirth explode in loud laughter.

"Omigod Ken! Can you believe that? Did I time travel or are we still in the 21st century?

That was unbelievable!"

"Maggie, do you really think our fathers um, discipline our mothers?"

"Not for a New York minute! I mean seriously? No way."

"But Amelia seemed very sure—"

"Well then maybe when they were newlyweds? I mean things were different thirty years ago."

"Are you going to ask your mother about it?"

"Well... I wasn't but, maybe I should? What about you?"

"Oh, I couldn't talk about something like that with my Mom, but I could tell my Dad what we've been told and see what he's got to say about it."

"And then we'll compare notes!" concludes Maggie and they exchange smiles.

The young couple are getting together after work for a drink and dinner the next day so they don't have a chance to speak until meeting at the restaurant. Ken is already there waiting when Maggie arrives.

"What kept you?" he asks.

"Oh work, again! you know how it is. As usual my boss acts surprised when the work day is over and always ends up wanting something done right at quitting time."

"Well, that's okay sometimes, Maggie, but you need to tell her *no* when we've got plans. We've talked about this before. I don't mind waiting for you when you've got a good reason, but I don't like it when your boss deliberately keeps you late. You aren't her only employee but you seem to be the only one she takes advantage of."

"Ugh, that's because the other girls are always out the door at the stroke of five and so I'm the one she catches and asks."

"Too bad. You need to stand up to her."

"Oh Ken I don't want to be a clock-watcher. I enjoy my job and I—"

"Maggie, I said no more."

"Well that's pretty damn bossy of you," she retorts. "I mean it's just you and me having dinner, it's not a special occasion or anything."

Ken narrows his eyes and stares at her until she starts fidgeting under his gaze.

Then he says: "I'm guessing you didn't speak to your Mom last night, but I had quite a talk with my father about our pre-marital counseling session. Frankly, he made me see things in a different light. He called my mother into the room to join the conversation. I was embarrassed to begin with, but neither of them were. That's because there's nothing sexual about home correction.

In fact, they went on to explain that spousal disciplining is simply a component of married life that just happens to involve whole or partial nudity for the wife. Not in a titillating way but only as a reinforcement to feel ashamed and penitent, and to fully experience the pain of the punishment."

"*To fully experience the pain*, Ken, can you hear yourself? Are you going to sit there and tell me you want to inflict pain on me? And shame?"

"No, you don't understand, Maggie. It's not something I *want* to do but that I *have* to do. For your sake, and for the sake of our marriage. For instance if we were married I would spank you for showing up late tonight."

"What!!??"

"I would, because I've told you before not to keep me waiting. Your boss is always asking for extra work from you but if you and I have plans you need to say no to her and meet me on time. If you don't, you'll be punished in order to learn how to behave properly."

"Behave properly? Really, Ken?"

"Yes, Maggie. It's important that you're respectful towards me, just as I always try to be respectful towards you. We're a partnership."

"Yeah, the kind where one of use is *more equal* than the other, right?"

"As the man, and head of the household, then yes I'm in charge. But Maggie, I love you so much, you know that..."

Standing, Maggie grabs hold of her purse and tells Ken:

"No, I'm really not sure I believe that anymore. I won't be staying for dinner." And turning she marches out of the restaurant.

Sitting in her car she waits for Ken. She allows him time to pay the bill and then expects to see him hurry out but he doesn't show up. After waiting much longer than she planned Maggie gives her head a shake and drives home, fuming all the way.

As soon as Maggie walks through the front door and catches sight of her mother the girl burst into tears.

"Oh Mom," she wails. "I don't think I can marry Ken after all." And then she is folded into the maternal embrace while sobbing.

Eventually the flow of tears dries enough that she can explain what happened. Her mother doesn't comment but keeps patting Maggie's hand to encourage her to continue.

After Maggie has gotten everything out she finishes by asking: "I had to leave, right Mom? What else could I do? If this is how Ken is going to treat me before we're even married then, well... I shouldn't marry him, right?"

"Maggie, I think you need to reconsider—"

But Maggie interrupts her mother crying out: "You wouldn't put up with that from Dad would you?"

"I would, I have, and I still do, Maggie. Your father and I have lived the DD lifestyle our whole married life. Actually, that's not quite true. As we got older, as you got older, we let it slide.

For a few years I was never corrected and then I started acting out and needed to be, as they say, *taken in hand*. I blame the perimenopause, it made me irritable and cranky, and I inflicted my bad moods on Dad.

Well he got fed up and rightly so but he manned up and ordered me to strip from the waist down and stick my nose in the corner until he was ready to deal with me.

Of course I tried to argue my way out of a spanking and it wasn't just from defiance. It was also from shame that my naked backside was no longer pert and firm. I'd had a baby, you, and I'd gotten older and fallen victim to gravity. But your father knew I needed to feel his dominance, that our marriage needed it, and so I was given a hard hand-spanking and put back in the corner to anticipate a follow-up with his belt.

By time he was finished cellulite was the least of my worries! but that spanking got me back on track. We both discovered that we'd let ourselves drift apart emotionally however after my punishment, with repeats as necessary, we have found our way back to each other, and our marriage is stronger than ever."

"Well I'm never going to allow a husband of mine to treat me like I'm a naughty child!"

"But that's exactly how you're behaving, Maggie. And children who behave badly often do so in order to feel the boundaries placed on them by loving discipline."

"Not me!"

"Ken phoned me from the restaurant and explained what happened. That's why I was waiting for you at the door, and that's why I invited him to come by. I heard his truck pull into the driveway so I think we should continue this talk with him. And your father, too."

The two men must have been listening outside the door because together they come into the room. Ken hurries over to Maggie and takes her hand. She tries to yank it back but he holds firm. Seeing him looking at her with such caring concern makes the tears well up again.

"Maggie, my sweet child," her father remains in the doorway and as he speaks her mother goes to stand beside him. He slings his arm across his wife's shoulders and the two of them look at their daughter with the same tender emotion Ken is showing.

"At times, every woman needs a bit of help to find her way. Some call it *attitude adjustment* but really it's just a helping hand, a firm hand, to steer you in the right direction. Your mother and I love you and want the very best for you. We're going to give you and Ken some privacy now and I'm sure you can work this out."

The older couple smile kindly before turning away, pulling the door closed behind them.

Ken draws Maggie's head against his chest and she slips her arms around his neck. Holding her tight he places gentle kisses on the crown of her head, his mouth moving down over her eyes, nose, and cheek before finding her lips. Maggie kisses him back eagerly.

They remain in each others arms for a few more minutes then Ken half-turns Maggie's body until she is laid across his lap. As soon as she realizes what he has in mind she begins to struggle but he's a strapping young man who works hard in a physical job and she is no match for his strength.

Taking hold of the hem of her dress he lifts it up to her waist. The sight of her panty-clad bottom made him pause for a moment in appreciation before he tamps down his lustful thoughts and concentrates on administering the kind of discipline his bride-to-be needs and, he now believes, craves. He understands that her naughty behavior has been a cry for his attention and her desperate need to be reassured of his devotion and concern.

Sliding his fingers into the waistband of her pastel panties he quickly pulls them down to bare her behind. His big hand immediately begins delivering a steady volley of spanks on her soft skin.

Maggie squirms and kicks, cursing at Ken, but he only increases the strength of each swat. Soon he's painted her smooth flesh a becoming shade of pink but knows he has a long way to go because his girl isn't submitting to her correction, she is fighting him with everything she has.

He sighs heavily, but secretly is enjoying his role as Maggie's teacher, guide, boss... and that reminds him of how she'd been late for their dinner because she put the wants of her boss ahead of his own. He berates her for this while increasing the tempo of his strokes and soon Maggie is squealing and twitching from the stinging smacks.

"Ken! Stop, please.. Ken, I won't.. I want.. please don't, it really hurts."

"You need to learn, Maggie, and it's up to me to teach you this lesson."

"No! I'm not a child, I'm a grown woman. Stop this right now!" she screeches in pain and anger.

Amazingly, Ken stops. Maggie scrambles to get up but he holds her firmly at his side while he half-stands to unbuckle his belt. She hears it whistle through the loops of his jeans and then he settles her bottom-up on his left thigh while he hooks his right leg over both of hers to hold them down.

Her awareness of just how helpless she is, how exposed and vulnerable, is both frightening and humiliating. Deep in her heart she knows Ken will never cause her real harm but she can't stop him from inflicting stinging pain. She just has to take whatever he decides she needs to be given.

Then she feels the burn as his belt lashes down on her sore, quivering backside and upper thighs. Ken steadily applies his punishing strokes up and down with each swat covering her from side to side. Soon every blessed inch of her is blisteringly hot and her complaints become wailing pleas. Still he continues because he knows how important her acceptance of this, his authority, is to their relationship.

When the moment comes that Maggie collapses, sobbing but compliant, Ken is relieved that the session is finally over. His girl has granted him the right of dominance and her own submission. Now he turns her to cradle in his arms, careful to keep her weight off of her well-spanked bottom.

He murmurs endearments while she cries wetly into the hollow of his throat. The door opens and Maggie's mother enters quietly with a bottle of lotion in her hand. She passes it to Ken without a word then leaves them alone again.

He slides Maggie over his shoulder and in that position is able to tenderly smooth the soothing aloe over her flaming flesh. He can feel the heat of her skin against his face and he praises her for being his very good girl who he loves deeply. Maggie, still crying, doesn't reply.

About ten minutes later Ken stands his worn-out fiancee on her feet and kissing her chastely on the lips he pulls up her panties, pulls down her dress, and leads her out of the room before sending her up to bed.

Her mother is there to help and her father is there to say goodnight to Ken and see him out. Shaking hands Maggie's Dad says *ouch!* and looking down Ken sees that the palm of his own hand is a solid red. Still warm, and that's from before the belting!

Ken doesn't feel any remorse, instead he's confident of having effectively made his point, and certain Maggie is reassured by his love.

At work the next morning Maggie discovers her willingness to put in long hours has paid off when she requests and receives an immediate transfer to Head Office.

She'd woken early despite having hardly slept. The night before found her tossing and turning for hours from the throbbing pain in her backside, the worries in her mind, and the ache in her heart. Getting up she packed her car with some clothes, wrote a note, and left everything else behind along with her engagement ring.

The End

Beta Has To Train His Alpha's Fated Mate

When Andrew comes into Logan's room he stops short and whistles at the sight of a beautifully shaped bottom sporting an even more beautiful shade of deep crimson. Standing in the corner bared from the waist down the rest of the package, showing a slim figure and long legs, is appealing but not nearly as enticing as the girl's glowing derriere.

"Beta!" cries the young woman in anguish, hearing that another man is present in the room.

"Oh get used to it, milady. Both Andrew and I are constantly in and out of our Alpha's chamber and I'm sure we'll find you in this exact same position on numerous occasions."

"Except that when Alexander is in residence his mate will be fully naked and he'll be the one reddening her bottom instead of you, Logan."

"And thank the Goddess for that reprieve. I could sprain my wrist administering this one's correction and she would still be wilful and naughty. My Alpha will have his hands full for the entire time of their mating, I have no doubt!"

"It sounds like her training is... difficult?"

"Well it's different because I'm training her to accept a spanking in the proper spirit, as a gift from her lord and master. But it's a constant battle for dominance and even though she loses every single time she still fights, refusing to submit with grace.

It's only because her family let her run wild and never gave her the true discipline all headstrong girls need. So, before Alexander comes home I need to get her used to being pulled across his lap for a thorough paddling on the bare.

In fact, come here Moraine and get across my knee again. You might as well get a taste of public punishment because Alexander won't hesitate to tame you whenever and wherever. You need to learn to take it with your chin up but your eyes downcast, never acknowledging the audience unless your Alpha orders you to do so."

Moraine comes forward slowly, reluctantly, and as soon as she gets within reach Logan grabs hold of her wrist and yanks her into position. He secures her legs by hooking his right over her ankles while lifting his left leg to raise her backside and expose her sit spot. He immediately begins applying a flurry of sharp smacks to that tender area, turning it an even more painful shade of red.

Andrew gets a good look at his petite new mistress. She's young with a very pretty face framed by wavy blonde hair down to her slender waistline. Moraine's nicely rounded bosom bounces unfettered against her shift each time she jerks or twitches at a stinging slap. She keeps her lips closed tight, struggling to remain silent and not plead for mercy.

The tuft of blonde hair that covers her vagina is very fair and the pink of her labia shows through. The young man feels a stirring in his groin and has to look away to repress his treasonous thoughts.

Moraine's squeaks and squeals of discomfort mean Logan has to speak loudly as he continues talking to Andrew saying:

"As the man responsible for disciplining our disobedient she-wolves, I'm always very firm – in fact, harsh – hoping it's just a one-time thing because this is work, not pleasure. I make it clear that I don't want to have them over my knee again so I give a very hard hand-spanking which is usually sufficient to keep them from any more misbehaving.

If it isn't, they'll get their second lesson with a longer spanking and then six painful lashes from my belt. Third lesson is twelve lashes, and the fourth lesson is eighteen hard strokes welting an already extremely sore, red bottom created from a prolonged hand-spanking. I've only needed to apply that punishment once and before you ask, yes, that stubborn brat was Felicity, just before she became my wife."

"I'm surprised she agreed to accept you after that!" chuckled Andrew.

"Well of course it's works differently when the spanking is between fated mates. There's a very pleasant sexual aspect involved. That's something neither Moraine nor I feel for each other so these sessions are real punishment for her and a tedious chore for me. She'll certainly know the difference when it's Alexander's hand raining down the blows. She'll be aroused, despite the sting, and he'll be maddened by her scent.

It's a fact that the Omega in a fated mate pairing cannot resist surrendering her body to her Alpha but her mind will fight for independence even as he calls her with his purr.

Poor Moraine. She won't be able to stop herself from provoking our Alpha into spanking her despite the pain of the punishment.

His need to crush that rebellious spirit again and again means plenty of over-the-knee correction followed by ravening passionate fucking and knotting."

"I do look forward to meeting the right she-wolf who I can claim in punishment and pleasure."

"Alexander will certainly combine both when he knots and marks this little virgin."

"Oh right! Oh she does have a lot in store, doesn't she?"

Moraine turns a tear-stained face of reproach towards Andrew but he doesn't notice, he's too entranced by the spectacle of her pretty bottom bouncing under Logan's steady spanks.

"She's taking that quite well, I think."

"You'd think so but we've been here before, haven't we Moraine? You see by the end of the day she's resigned to her discipline but come morning she'll be full of spicy sass and I'll have to wear my poor hand down tanning her poor bottom all over again."

"How many days have you been in training?"

"This is day four and I think we'll have two more days before Alexander gets here. I'm spanking her several times a day, starting with her fighting mad in the morning – kicking her legs and calling me names – then sobbing herself into exhaustion at her afternoon session. This is her second spanking this evening and I expect we're done for today.

Honestly my hand gets sore and it's hard and callused so I'm quite sure her behind is just scorching."

"May I?" asks Andrew and Logan nods permission. The younger man reaches over to lay his palm on the girl's smooth red globes. "She's blisteringly hot!" he says in awe and admiration of Logan's skill.

"What do you say, Moraine?" Logan demands.

Flushing with embarrassment she answers in a low voice: "Thank you for the compliment, Andrew."

"And what do you say to me?"

With a deep sigh Moraine replies: "Thank you for my training Logan. I appreciate learning how to please my Alpha."

"Tomorrow we'll be working on your inner thighs and you'll really feel that," says Logan as he caresses her tender, quivering cheeks. "I've been instructed that on the last day your Alpha wants you primed and prepped for his homecoming. That means we need to present him with an appealing salmon-pink bottom that he can quickly turn scarlet red.

I honestly don't know if that will adequately prepare you for sex with Alexander but at least you'll become deeply aroused while you're across his knee. He'll enjoy inspecting every inch of you! and you'll have the pleasurable aspect of sexual gratification to help ease your pain."

He sends her back to her corner with a warning not to rub her bottom.

Both men study her flaming backside while sniffing her scent, faint but unmistakable. Her body is learning how to respond. Andrew sighs deeply while Logan just massages his spanking hand.

"It would be easier if I could give her a taste of leather but there's no belting the Alpha's mate, that privilege is his alone."

The End

Sent To The Headmaster For a Hard Lesson

Opening the door to the anteroom Headmaster Chivers spies the girl sitting on the bench biting her nails. She straightens up when she sees him and gives her head a toss, feigning indifference.

Now in her senior year he sees that she's grown into a beautiful young woman. While technically an adult she's still a student under his control. He gives an anticipatory smirk, enjoying his power while savoring her downfall.

"Come into my study, Miss Marsh." He holds the door open and waits for her to go in.

Motioning her to stand before his desk he walks purposely around it to sit in the big leather chair, clasping his hands and waiting patiently. Tilting his head, his expression mild, he surveys her from head to toe.

They remain in silence for a couple of minutes and Headmaster Chivers secretly admires the girl's defiant poise. Looking her up and down he sees rebellion in her eyes, in her facial expression, in her posture, and in the way she has adulterated her school uniform.

Her tie is pulled low, the top couple of blouse buttons are undone, her skirt is so short it must be rolled up at the waist, knee socks are conspicuously absent, and she's removed the laces from her saddle shoes.

Aimee Marsh is very pretty but she'll turn into an unhappy, spoiled, and discontented woman unless she's taken firmly in hand now. Before it's too late, he thinks.

Her figure has already blossomed and Headmaster Chivers suspects she's wearing a black bra but doesn't want to look too closely. Miss Marsh is here to be punished, not seduced. And not to be a seducer, either!

"Your teachers report that they're at their wits' end. And it's a unanimous complaint—"

"Even Mr Clough?" she boldly interrupts.

Headmaster Chivers makes a note to look into the Music Teacher's reputation and behavior. Miss Marsh's comment sounds suspiciously personal.

"I said unanimous... please, don't interrupt again."

The girl scowls and crosses her arms over her chest. *Oh yes definitely a favored little madam,* he silently chuckles.

"You do know the proper pose to assume when being addressed by any adult in this school don't you, Miss Marsh?"

Rolling her eyes the girl unclasps her arms and puts them behind her back, one hand holding the opposite wrist. With a sly smile she pulls her shoulders back and thrusts her chest forward then watches closely to see where his gaze settles.

However Headmaster Chivers stands up and walks around her, not saying a word. She soon gets fidgety under his scrutiny. She might be eighteen but she's still only a girl, after all.

"In addition to being a place for me to work and relax, my study, as I'm sure you're aware, is also a place of punishment. Corporal punishment. Errant students are summoned here to be disciplined because young ladies seem to need some harsh, physical correction from time to time."

Miss Marsh doesn't reply or even acknowledge his words but her body has stiffened and he can tell that she's listening intently. Suddenly he swoops in and grabbing her by the arms drags the girl over to an odd-looking piece of upholstered leather furniture in the far corner. It looks a bit like the vaulting horse they use for gymnastics, but shorter.

Moving quickly but with assurance Headmaster Chivers pulls Miss Marsh over the apparatus and buckles both of her wrists into leather cuffs. She's now in a bent-over position with her backside pointing up at about the level of his waist.

He flips up her plaid skirt and tut-tuts over the lacy black underwear she has on. Definitely not part of the school's uniform, and another example of this little minx breaking the rules to suit herself.

Reaching up he yanks the skirt free of its folds and slips it off her. He hesitates, as though contemplating whether or not to let her keep her panties on and he hears her intake of breath... but of course a clad bottom was never going to be allowed. Her panties follow the skirt down her legs and over her feet to be tossed aside.

She murmurs something in protest.

"Oh speak up, Miss Marsh. In fact scream if you like. I'm certain you will be screaming soon enough. Don't worry that anyone will hear you because *of course* they will hear you! and the teachers will all smile with satisfaction when they do. Even Mr Clough.

The students might spare you a sympathetic thought but even that's rather unlikely, isn't it? Not after all the complaints I've received about your bullying."

After taking a good look at his half-naked captive Headmaster Chivers walks round to the front of the contraption and fiddles with a wooden block which he unscrews and pushes into position just under Miss

Marsh's chin, forcing her head back so that he can see her upturned face. He tightens the screw to hold her in place.

When she closes her eyes he chuckles, saying: "Open your eyes. I would think you'd want to have a look at the implements I'm going to use in your *behavior adjustment lesson.*"

Assuming a lecturing tone he states: "There's anecdotal evidence that Galileo Galilei claims *seeing the instruments laid out for his torture was all it took to make him recant his heresy.* I'm afraid that you aren't being given the option to recant, confess, or atone. Your punishment is inevitable but I will admit these tools are quite scary. So, let me tell you all about them. I think that even when the news is bad it's still always best to know, don't you agree?"

Miss Marsh opens her eyes and gives him a wary look. He's noticed her surreptitiously testing her bonds and he smirks at her dismay when she realizes she's truly trapped. The longer she's held in this position with her buttocks bared, her chin raised, and her wrists secured the more he can see her defiance melting away. Instead he sees anxiety creeping in.

"The girls attending here these last few years must have been very well-behaved students because I never realized that during the clean-up from the leaky roof flooding our spanking implements got damaged or lost. Maybe stolen as souvenirs?" he muses. "Hmm, hardly fond memories..."

"Therefore, this school doesn't have a wooden paddle for paddling or a cane for caning. But I have an inventive turn of mind Miss Marsh, and have put together an assortment of tools to teach you the hard lesson I've been asked to impart on your bare bottom."

He turns to a table under the window that holds various items. Miss Marsh can't see them clearly so he obligingly holds them up to the light.

As he picks up each implement he lovingly fondles its fabric while giving a brief description.

"First, a wooden spoon from the kitchen. It's a solid piece and the bowl of the spoon gives a nice smack." He slaps it into his palm a few times so she can hear and understand the effect.

"Next we have two belts – one thin, the other thick, both leather and both long enough to get a good swing going." He wraps a fist around each belt and whistles them through the air. "These will stripe you nicely."

He notices out of the corner of his eye that her whole body is trembling in fear and anticipation.

"Naturally, the school supplies don't include whips or floggers but I'm rather proud of this little beauty." He holds us a length of thick, hairy rope with knots interspersed at two or three inch intervals.

"I've made three of these and if I hold them together like this I can do this." He demonstrates with a mighty swing against the table and the tool slashes down with a loud thwack. "Those knots are going to leave marks," he adds happily.

"Finally, this is a truly inspired piece, based on me reading old-time books as a boy. In those stories whenever someone got punished they had a switch taken to their backsides. Often the young miscreant was forced to go cut and strip one or two themselves, adding to the cruelty of their whipping.

So, I had a wander in the grounds and got this from one of the willow trees. I just had to strip off the leaves although it is still a bit knobby. It's long enough so I can really put some power into my swing and thin enough to raise welts on your tender skin."

As he swishes the switch around with its whistling sound Miss Marsh loses all pretense of dignity. She bursts into tears and twists and turns her hips futilely struggling to escape. Once she realizes she is well and truly caught she kicks her feet and shouts in temper. She's helpless and terrified.

Headmaster Chivers approaches her with the wooden spoon and begins applying sharp taps up and down, and side to side, all over her bare bottom. He increases the tempo and comments on how pink her skin is turning.

"Does this sting, Miss Marsh?" he asks with the smile evident in his voice.

The girl doesn't answer so he brings the spoon down much harder and she gasps out her reply: "Yes it does sting! It really stings!"

"Is that the proper way to address me, Miss Marsh?"

"No Headmaster. Sorry, Sir."

"Wayward females, girls and women both, thrive on correction. The whole point of their naughty behavior is to call a man's attention to them. It's a cry for help, they want a firm hand to guide them back on the right track. We have to hope they'll find a man with the moral fiber to give them the punishment they crave in a manner that douses the flame of their rebellion.

In this school that job falls to me, and I take this duty entrusted to me seriously."

By now Miss Marsh is sobbing uncontrollably. Stepping back a few paces Headmaster Chivers can see the girl's red face and her reddening bottom. He replaces the spoon on the table and picks up the thin belt. Making sure that the buckle is fully covered within his fist he doubles it up and swings it with a loud crack on her flesh. Two strokes.

Miss Marsh gives a high-pitched scream each time from the pain.

Headmaster Chivers now switches over to the thick belt and performs the same act. This time Miss Marsh shouts out at each of the two lashings.

Headmaster Chivers continues, giving the girl two strokes with his knotted ropes – those thuddy blows make the lower half of her body convulse – and two swishes with the switch. She shrieks even louder at those cutting stings.

"Well Miss Marsh, now that you've had a taste of each spanking tool which is your preference? What implement would you like me to continue with?"

"None Headmaster! Please-please-please-please don't spank me anymore. Please don't, I promise to be good."

"Hmm, I'm not hearing as much conviction as I'd like. Perhaps some hand-spanking will help focus your thoughts."

Headmaster Chivers is pleased to see that the implements have added color but no welts or stripes to his charge's tender flesh. He has no intention of brutalizing her but he definitely wants her *sore and sorry*. The Headmaster is happy to let her think she's being beaten far worse then she actually is.

Of course he's not going to hold back from using his hand as firmly as possible. He proceeds to thoroughly smack Miss Marsh's exposed skin from the top of her round bottom right down across her upper thighs. While working the whole area into a uniform blushing red he recites her crimes and extracts her promises to stop being bad and start being good.

"Insolence, disobedience, insubordination—"

"Oh please Sir, I'll do better. I will, I promise!"

"Bullying, name-calling, swearing, fighting—"

"No more, please! I won't do anything like that ever again!"

"Unfinished homework, sloppy classroom work, talking in class—"

"Oh Headmaster! Oh, Sir please, I'm begging you, please stop!"

"At your age you should be setting an example for the younger students."

"I will, pl-please Sir I promise, I will!"

Miss Marsh is gasping for breath between her crying and her pleading. Headmaster Chivers surveys his handiwork and decides she won't soon forget this lesson but... a dozen more spanks will highlight his point. Her naked behind is now glowing.

What her punishment has lacked in severity it more than makes up for in fear. She probably feels like she's taken a dozen strokes with each item when it's only been two apiece, except for the wooden spoon and his hard hand.

"I'm going to finish for now... but I'm leaving you on display in this position to contemplate your wrongdoing, and so that I can consider if... well... hmmm."

Headmaster Chivers settles down in the chair behind his desk to contemplate Miss Marsh and instill in her the fear that he might decide to strike again.

He murmurs in a voice loud enough to carry: "Is that enough, I wonder? Maybe I should deliver another... hmmm."

He can tell she's holding her breath in fearful anticipation.

"I know!" he exclaims as if a new thought has occurred. "There are a couple of teachers who will appreciate the opportunity to inspect your red bottom and who, I'm sure, can advise me if I've administered sufficient correction."

The girl renews her crying and begging not to be exposed and humiliated any further but Headmaster Chivers turns a deaf ear to her entreaties. He leaves the room and returns a few minutes later accompanied by the elderly English teacher and the middle-aged French teacher. These two women were the most vocal in their complaints against their badly behaved student.

Madame Beaupre has never been able to control her classroom and Miss Marsh led the other girls in all kinds of mischief that drove the woman mad. She looks at Miss Marsh's tear-streaked face and well-spanked bottom and gives a nod of satisfaction saying: "Bon."

"Oh! Do you really think so, Madame? Personally I would advise more." Miss Aylesworth surprises Headmaster Chivers with her comment because she's such a gentle soul. "I'm not satisfied that Miss Marsh is contrite enough, and believe it will be beneficial to prolong her punishment. Just to be absolutely certain she truly has learned her lesson."

"NO! No, don't you dare listen to that old bitch—" screams out Miss Marsh in a panic before realizing she's played right into her English teacher's hands – or rather, the headmaster's!

Madame Beaupre gasps aloud at the outburst.

"You're obviously correct in your assessment, Miss Ayelsworth, and I defer to your superior knowledge of teenaged girls," replies Headmaster Chivers with relish in his voice.

"Oh no please, please! No more! I'm sorry, really I am, I didn't mean it. Please don't."

Completely ignoring the desperate girl Headmaster Chivers invites the teachers to have a look at his collection of implements and give their opinion on which tool to use to continue the disciplining.

"Oh look a switch! I remember being switched by my dear Papa when I was a naughty girl. That's a lesson you never forget."

"One vote for the switch, then, and what do you say Madame?"

In her heavily accented English the woman points to the thicker of the two belts and suggests she'd like to see the girl wear some bright stripes on her red bottom.

"Well Ladies, both are good options and I can't choose between them so I'll deliver three more strokes from each. Those six new lines should finish this chastisement off nicely. Please stay and witness Miss Marsh get the full treatment."

"That she deserves! Monsieur."

"That she has *earned,* Headmaster."

The stricken girl cries out piteously: "No, no more. Please, please I beg you..." but her pleading is in vain.

Headmaster Chivers doesn't waste any time before laying down three painful lashes with the belt. These matching stripes, well-spaced, show deep red against the girl's already colorful buttocks. He pauses a moment so the pain can settle before letting her really feel the sting of the switch.

"Four! Five! Six!" he calls out as he slashes the switch in three whistling, whipping strokes. He's managed to fill the two spaces between the three stripes and finished with a diagonal line across all five.

Miss Marsh's shrieking sobs are so loud he can barely hear Miss Ayleworth compliment him on the finesse of his placement.

The elderly teacher comes closer for a good long look. Chuckling, she opines that this girl will endure a lifetime of home correction at the hand of her future husband.

Madame simply smiles with grim satisfaction and the two teachers leave the room.

Headmaster Chivers stands beside the helpless girl as if considering yet more but after about five minutes he gathers up her skirt and panties, releases her from the punishment bench, and tells her to get dressed as she is free to go. She practically jumps into her skirt, doesn't bother with her panties, and scurries to the door but his voice stops her:

"What are you forgetting, Miss Marsh?"

She stops, confused, since he's already excused her then realizes what he wants to hear. With her head bowed but in a clear voice she tells him:

"Thank you for my lesson, Headmaster."

Epilogue:

Miss Aylesworth sits in a rocking-chair holding a chubby baby while in the bedroom next door to the nursery the elderly lady can hear a woman squealing and squawking at being soundly spanked.

"Years ago I predicted that your Mummy would earn frequent bare bottom punishments and my nephew, your Daddy, is just the man to take her in hand. She's such a lucky girl and not in the least bit penitent."

The End

That String Bikini

She juts out her chin in defiance saying: "My bikini is not *scandalous* like you claim so I'm wearing it. I don't care what you think, you're not my father."

Deliberately keeping my voice low and rumbly I tell her: "Go change into something else right now or you'll be soundly spanked, is that what you want?"

Anger flashes in her eyes as she forms her lips into an exaggerated pout sarcastically squealing: "Oooh! Doesn't that sound like sexy fun!"

"Oh it will be! *for me*. For you? not so much because it's punishment." I'm standing close enough to feel her thighs clench.

"That's a stupid punishment for a grown woman." she sulks, tossing her head and placing her hands on her hips.

"But perfect for a silly little girl who's acting like a spoiled brat."

"Am not!"

I can't help but smirk as I pull her across my knee... after all *she asked for it!*

Resting my hands on her bikini-clad bottom I lightly tap my fingers to awaken her nerve endings. I know this little vixen will drown in her own self-induced arousal from my words alone. Her heightened anticipation will make punishing her quivering flesh even more delicious. I tamp down my own rising libido in order to draw out my pleasure.

"Tut-tut, you're such a mouthy little brat, aren't you? And in dire need of a heavy-handed spanking from your man. Mmm-hmm, it's time to teach this naughty little bottom a lesson. I'm sure you'll be a good obedient girl once your backside is burning.

How shameful, to be manhandled into this position and punished like a child. Unless... oh! Maybe you weren't properly disciplined as a little girl? I bet that's it. Having met your nice Daddy I'm sure you never got the tanning you deserved.

That explains why you've manoeuvred yourself over my lap, presenting yourself for a good old-fashioned bare-bottomed spanking. Begging for it, in fact."

She squeals in protest but I simply repeat myself, reinforcing the tantalizing promise of that phrase: "Yes sweet cheeks, you're going to get the bare-bottomed spanking you've earned... and want. Let's just pull these down so I can get a good look at the pristine canvas I'll be working on."

My words are driving her to a frenzy of squirming as she struggles, ineffectively, to free herself. I draw her bikini bottoms down to her knees and allow myself plenty of time to admire her trembling mounds.

"Oh yes, I'm going to have fun painting this gorgeous derriere a blushing pink. You'll fight against your... *correction* but I'll enjoy every wiggle and every yelp. You'll entertain me with such a delightful spectacle while my firm hand keeps applying stroke after stroke, smack after smack, until you've been given the thorough spanking you need."

"No! No!" she gasps, but the undulations of her hips as she presses her core against the muscles of my thigh belie her words and entice me even more.

"Oh yes, my dirty little girl. And when your bum is tender to the touch and bright pink to the eye I'll slip my hand between your legs and then? My fingers will tickle their way through your wet folds into your tight little hole. My thumb will strum your clit until your hips are jerking to chase your orgasm. What a show you're gonna put on for me!"

I begin the spanking and her pale skin colors up quickly with my crisp smacks. Her drawn-out groan is music to my cock. But first I educate her in the meaning of true dominance.

"And then I'll stop diddling your pussy. You'll cry out in frustration wiggling your groin, trying to find my fingers again, but I'll have to explain that you can't have an orgasm until you beg me to continue your spanking – harder and faster."

"No! Never!" she insists but I chuckle at her feeble defiance.

I remind her again: "You are utterly helpless pinned across my knee, your pretty ass so tempting and vulnerable. Such a plump bottom is made for a disciplinarian's pleasure! I will spank these mounds over and over and over again.

You will kick your legs and swear and shriek and scream at me but I won't stop. I'll give you much more than you think you can take baby girl but you *will* take it because it's what you need and giving it to you is what I want.

I'm going to take my time to stretch out my fun and excitement. Honestly, embarrassing you like this will give me such satisfaction." I let my voice drop down to the growly rumble that always turns her on as I add: "Especially since I know how exquisitely you'll suffer in humiliation."

I reach the point of marking her a deep pink sooner than I expected. Resting my hand I savor the heat warming my palm from her punished flesh. I massage the reddened skin before delivering the promised clit play. She's soaking wet, confirming my surmise that she's the type of woman who revels in physical domination against her will. Blameless, because she's helpless. Weak, because I'm strong.

I decide then and there that my bratty girlfriend is going to become my wife. My well-disciplined wife.

Her breathy moans soon turn into shallow pants signaling her impending climax so I stop and am rewarded with a wail of dismay.

Chuckling, I remind her what she needs to do next. "If you want me to give you an orgasm you first need to beg me to finish your spanking, remember? C'mon now, let's hear the words from those pouty lips in that sulky mouth."

"Unngghh!" she snarls, but I don't budge. I just let my exhales blow down on her quivering goosebumped flesh. She swivels her hips trying to find friction for her engorged clit against my semi-hard cock until I comment that she's certainly presenting a pretty picture of a dirty, desperately horny slut.

Still she keeps her lips pressed tight against telling me what I want to hear.

I hum while letting my fingernails lightly scrape across her primed and stimulated skin, showing her that I'm relaxed and patient and fully in control of my body and hers.

With a frustrated burst of air she finally says: "Oh go ahead, and do what you want, you're going to do it anyway."

"Hmm, that's a very poor attempt at begging my needy whore. You're going to have to do much better than that."

"Fuck you!"

I laugh out loud which only makes her pummel my leg with her clenched fists. She's angry and too sore to want another spanking, but too turned on to refuse it.

"I'll help you out, okay? Let's see you can begin by describing how ashamed of yourself you are—"

"I'm not! I've done nothing wrong!"

"Well actually you've disrespected me, refused to change, and then failed to apologize for your sassy behavior. That makes you a bad girl, but the real shame must come from the wet mess you've made of your perfect little cunt. All because I spanked your bare bottom raw."

That phrase again, it's elicited an involuntary twitch that my eye catches with satisfaction.

"No, that's not... I didn't... I don't..."

"Just tell me, sweetie. Repeat after me: *please sir, I need more spanking.*"

The longest pause ensues and it's like I can hear her thoughts, hear the conflict going on in her brain, as evidenced by her tense body and flexing limbs.

At last, in a quavery quiet voice she asks: "Please sir, spank me again."

Naturally I'm tempted to tease and say *what? Please repeat that, I can't hear you* but instead I give her another prompt: "Show me that you want to please me by telling me to keep spanking until *I* decide you've learned your lesson."

Now I hear the tears in her voice as she says: "I.. please.. I need you to spank me as much as you want..." her voice trails off in a sob.

I wait a full minute, forcing myself to be patient, until I see her body start to tremble as she lifts her hips raising her delectable ass in invitation. She's fearful of the pain but hopeful for the pleasure and I am not going to disappoint my woman in either regard.

My hand comes down in a barrage of sharp spanks as I pattern her bottom and upper thighs with my handprints until the whole area turns a solid hot-red color. My misbehaving brat sure knows who the boss is now!

She's bucking her hips and flailing about with her arms and legs, desperately trying to evade the stinging spanks. Wailing in pain, way past embarrassment, just desperately begging me to stop and claiming she'll be *my best good girl ever.*

I need to push her that little bit further so I keep going until her entire body falls limp, arms sagging to the ground and her thighs falling open. After that it only takes a couple of seconds worth of me pinching her clit before she explodes in ecstasy.

She's so much smaller than me I can easily shift her around, pushing her head-first down to the floor between my legs. Holding on to her hips I lift her up to bring her shiny wet cunt to my lips. She's so wet with desire happily giving me a tangy taste of her cum that's thick as honey and smooth as cream. Again she orgasms but I keep assaulting her sensitive clit with my tongue until she screams my name in yet another outburst of pleasure.

Hooking an arm around her waist I draw her up against my chest, loving how she's so petite against my muscular frame, and quickly freeing my cock I plunge deep, sliding easily into her slick channel. The heat of her well-spanked ass draws my eyes down and I admire the sight of my cock sliding in and out under her tender bum. I feel an overpowering domineering urge to always keep her bottom burning red. This is how my naughty girl should look all the time.

Moving my arm up I push her bikini bra out of my way and squash her round tits into my hand. I move back and forth across her chest tweaking first one hard nipple and then the other, again and again. My other hand grips her hip holding her firmly in place while I drive my cock rhythmically in and out, in and out, until we both reach our peak together.

She makes a kittenish mewling sound, worn out from her multiple orgasms and her spanking.

When our breathing slows I turn her body around to cuddle my sweetheart in my arms as I tightly embrace my complacently submissive girl. Tilting her chin up I brush the tears from her face before planting a loving kiss on her puffy lips.

For the next couple of days my cock will twitch with satisfaction every time I see her shift uncomfortably while sitting down. Now she knows that the sight of her sexy body is for my eyes only... and the consequences if she disobeys.

"Mine," I declare and she confirms that with a sweetly contented sigh.

The End

Warden Gives Inmate a Parting Gift

The Warden is reviewing his file on Prisoner 5872. He never actually met her in the 28 months she was incarcerated in this penitentiary which is a shame because she looks really hot in her mug shot.

Although he would have seen her paraded by while shackled to the other prisoners on the day she was transported in, he certainly didn't notice her then. Now, they're going to have a face-to-face interview before he signs her passport to freedom and he's looking forward to it.

Just under a year ago the Warden's wife left him and the divorce has already been finalized. She said she didn't commit a crime and shouldn't have to live in a prison. They actually have a nice bungalow on the grounds but, technically, they are still within the fenced area and the penitentiary is in an isolated spot of the state.

He sees her point but nevertheless the Warden is feeling hard-done-by, and hasn't been feeling favorably disposed towards women for some time now.

The Warden's secretary shows Prisoner 5872 in. Her accompanying guard has remained in the anteroom. The Warden gestures for Prisoner 5872 to take a seat and then comes around his desk to sit on the edge and look down at her.

"You haven't been in this office of mine before, have you?"

"No, Warden."

"Hmmm, you must have been a model prisoner during your stay."

"Thank you, Warden."

"Yes, well. That's a highly unusual state of affairs. Of course your time here has been considerably less than what most of our... what should I call them? *Guests* isn't right and neither is *Clients* and some of them will never be just *Visitors...*" he smiles at her adding: "Bit of a conundrum, isn't it?"

"How about calling them inmates?"

"Oh my, I think that sounds a little sassy coming from such a perfect prisoner!"

"Sorry, Warden."

"Sorry, eh? You certainly seem obedient and submissive but I have to wonder. Hmmm. Anyhow, as I was saying, practically every *inmate* here has needed to spend some time in this office being disciplined by me. It's simply a fact of life that at some point all female prisoners are going to need to be taken in hand."

Her eyes widen and he's pleased to see she recognizes that phrase.

Changing his cajoling tone to a more serious one The Warden continues saying: "You've applied for early release based on your record of good conduct here."

"Yes, Warden."

"Granting this is entirely at my discretion."

There's a noticeable pause before Prisoner 5872 nods and answers: "Yes, Warden."

"Well, I'm inclined to say...hmmm." He stops and appears to be thinking but Prisoner 5872 is quite sure he's pretending.

"I think *every* resident in my prison should have a taste of what discipline awaits rule-breakers. Now in your 28 months in my custody you, apparently, haven't broken any rules but... I find that hard to believe. I suspect you just weren't caught. Or perhaps you're a favorite of one *or more* of the guards?"

Prisoner 5872 hasn't responded or reacted but he can see that she's listening intently.

"So, I propose that you submit to my correction – a lighter-than-normal correction since it hasn't been *proven* that you deserve punishment – and then I could consider releasing you early with a clear conscience, knowing I've done what I can to discourage you from ever being sent back."

"And if I don't submit?"

Inwardly she's cursing at herself for leaving out his title because it shows she's in a temper but she can't believe she's being backed into a corner like this.

"Warden, Sir," she quickly adds.

Although he's definitely noticed the slight and her resentment he gives no sign. The truth is he's enjoying her predicament - her disappointment and frustration - while realization sets it.

Spreading his hands wide he replies: "No problem at all, Prisoner 5872. You'll go back to your cell and in four... it *is* four more months, right? You'll have served your full term and be released anyhow."

"So you're saying early release is not an option? Warden?"

"Oh, it's an option Prisoner 5872, but it's up to you to decide whether or not your going to choose it."

"Decide between submitting to your correction now or waiting four more months to be released."

"Well, hopefully it will only be *just* the four more. I mean, any serious infraction – like fighting with a guard or another prisoner – will definitely extend your stay."

Whole sentences of words filled with emotion silently pass between them as they hold each other's gaze. She knows he'll set her up and he knows she knows that.

"And," he adds brightly, "You'd be disciplined then anyhow. Real punishment, too."

"Warden, it seems you hold the high hand in this card game."

He bends forward with a cold smile saying: "And it's a heavy hand that I will wield firmly."

Prisoner 5872 shudders at the implied threat but feels she has no choice, she has to agree to his terms. There's no question that a bout of corporal punishment is worth avoiding four more months in this place.

The Warden walks back around his desk and pressing the intercom announces to his secretary that he's not to be disturbed.

"Yes Sir," she replies, adding: "I'm already holding your calls."

"You've got her well-trained, haven't you Warden?" asks Prisoner 5872 no longer bothering with any pretense of obedience.

The Warden gives her a wide smile and replies "It took a lot of work to get that girl trained just exactly how I want. Most of it was pleasurable – for me, not her - but, she's a lifer so it was worth the effort."

Walking past Prisoner 5872 he goes to the door and locks it, then returns to his desk and flips a couple of switches. Prisoner 5872 sees the red lights over the two cameras go out. There will be no more surveillance until The Warden is done.

Next he clears the items off the coffee-table and pulls it away from the divan. He flicks a lever in the arm of the sofa and the back drops down to make a bed.

He directs Prisoner 5872 to come over by the bed while he sits on the coffee-table in front of her.

"I'm going to give you a series of orders and I don't want to see any hesitation or hear any complaints. Just do what you're told and your... *ordeal* will soon be over. Do you understand?"

"Yes, Warden."

"Good. Of course that's what they all say yet still I hear arguments and have to deal with stubborn disobedience but you seem to be an intelligent girl so we'll see.

Since this isn't a punishment discipline I'm going to add some pleasure to the proceedings. Pain and pleasure combine to heighten experiences exquisitely, don't you think?"

"So I get the pain and you get the pleasure?"

"Aha! There's the feisty girl I knew was hiding under that demure exterior. I like that – to an extent.

Okay, first remove all of your clothes - I do mean everything - and do it nice and slow so I can enjoy watching."

Despite her urge to rebel Prisoner 5872 knows she has to comply. She doesn't dance for him but she does undress with a few exaggerated movements that make him smile in appreciation.

Once she's naked he motions for her to turn around and he comments on what he's seeing while he takes a good look.

"Nice high breasts with little pink nipples. They're really small, aren't they? Rub them inmate, and get them hard and red. That's right, now flick them with your fingers. Yes, yes just like that. Keep doing it, I want to see them swell. Yeah, that's good.

Now turn around again and let me study that ass. Mmm-hmm, round and plump. Very nice. Grab your ankles so I can have a peek inside your anus. Oh what a tight puckered rose! I wish I'd been present for your cavity search. Yes, we might get back to that later, we'll see.

Face forward again and spread your legs, no sit down first. Scoot up to the edge of the bed and now spread your legs really wide. Wider. Okay, I've got a front-row seat for a private audience," he chuckles.

"Now start playing with yourself and I want to see that clit of yours get all wet and shiny."

How can I get aroused when all I want to do is slap that stupid smirk off your stupid face? thinks Prisoner 5872, angry and frustrated at the helpless, hopelessness of her situation. She know she's hesitating too long and casts about in her mind for something erotic to think of, anything to stimulate her so she can masturbate quickly.

While thinking she starts fondling her breasts then lets her head drop back while running her hands up her throat along her scalp and through her hair. That gives her shivers that goosebump her skin.

It's about three years since she's been with a man. She imagines a strong, muscular guy – a bad boy type but nevertheless the kind who makes you feel safe and secure in his arms. Her eyes have closed and her mouth has opened. She lets one hand stretch across both breasts while the other is lazily drawing circles on her belly as it drifts downwards.

She slips a finger deep in the folds of her private place then slowly draws it up until she feels the tingle in her clit. There's wetness and she starts to slide her finger back and forth over the hard little nub. Unawares she's drawn up her legs to push her vagina forward and that's when the Warden claps his hands, bringing her out of her reverie.

"That's very good my dear, but no orgasms allowed! At least not yet. I enjoyed that little show you put on for me and I can see, hear, and smell your arousal. It's been quite some time since you got fucked, hasn't it? So now that we've both had some pleasure, well I'm afraid it's time for you to experience some pain."

Feeling a bit disoriented and frustrated after her interrupted climax Prisoner 5872 follows the Warden with her eyes. He walks to the far end of the bed and pats it with the instruction that she's supposed to approach on her hands and knees.

She follows his instructions and being such a big man he easily pulls her into the position he wants. She's facing a wall with a full-length mirror and is distracted by the sight of herself, naked and bleary-eyed, kneeling on the bed.

The Warden walks in front of her, blocking her view, and reaching down quickly snaps her wrists into the leather restraints attached to the divan. Her arms are pulled wide apart and this drags down her shoulders and head. He pushes her knees closer to the top of the bed forcing her hips to lift high. There is a strap on each side that he uses to secure her legs, just above the knee, pulling them wide apart too.

Prisoner 5872 looks in the mirror to see herself sprawled awkwardly with her bottom in the air which must mean her vagina is fully exposed, and her breasts swing as they hang down.

The Warden gives a little giggle as he approaches the bed carrying a leather paddle. It's about the size of a ping-pong paddle but there's some flex to it. He's taken off his suit jacket and now her eyes drop to the groin area of his pants but she sees no telltale signs of arousal.

"You are pretty as a picture right now Prisoner 5872 but I promise I'll only give you a taste of my discipline although I'm sorely tempted..."

And with that he applies the first stroke. It's hard and it's very painful. The suppleness of the leather means he can follow through on his swing instead of being stopped on a thuddy impact with her flesh. Prisoner 5872 can't help herself, it stings so much she yowls. The Warden immediately delivers another smack with a backhanded stroke.

He continues swinging back and forth, back and forth, each contact burning a trail across her bare flesh. She can hear him breathing heavily and then he begins murmuring angry little sounds of satisfaction that develop into words:

"This is what a naughty bitch needs and I'm giving it to her... this hot ass is on fire! I'll spank her until she understands how to be a good wi—woman. Christ, I'm sure doing a number on this pretty little rear. The cunt sure has this coming, and I'll teach her to fuck with me."

Through the haze of pain Prisoner 5872 realizes she's being used as the whipping boy for someone else in the Warden's mind. She figures it's probably his ex-wife, there had been plenty of gossip in the cells about his failed marriage and how bad-tempered he'd become since the divorce went through.

He tosses the paddle aside and begins peppering her red skin with the heavy hand he'd threatened her with earlier. Covering all the areas the paddle missed until every inch, practically down to her knees, is painfully burning.

By now Prisoner 5872 is sobbing, her face wet with her tears and screwed up in agony. Looking in the mirror again she catches him greedily looking from her face to her bottom which is reflected back, and she is shocked to see it's fiery red color. The Warden is smiling, pleased at this evidence of what he's done, proud of his brutal punishment.

He steps back and she can see that his aroused cock is bulging against his pants now. Masturbation and nudity didn't excite him but hurting her certainly has.

He picks up something off his desk and when he turns back towards his captive the gleeful look on his face frightens her. With a menacing expression he lifts up the device in his hand and flips a switch. It's a vibrator. She knows he won't apply it in a way she'll enjoy.

The almost-orgasmic state Prisoner 5872 was left in after her self-pleasuring vanished during the vicious paddling. Now the vibrator is applied against her sensitive but dry clit and it brings agony.

Fortunately the Warden doesn't leave it there but instead strokes up and down between her lips then starts probing into her hole. He pushes it in a little further and then further still. Now he's stroking in and out, going faster and deeper, and when he pushes it up against her clit again the buzzing vibration made her explode in a painful orgasm.

She hears the Warden laugh with delight and realizes this is just one more way for him to dominate and humiliate. He loves the power he wields over her unwilling body. She's so tightly bound it's impossible to escape his invading hands.

Prisoner 5872 barely stops trembling when he attacks her delicate flesh once again. Her nub is overly sensitive but also very wet so at least the lubrication protects her from friction this time.

Again he penetrates her with his toy and there's nothing she can do to prevent him – she's totally exposed, wide open and vulnerable. He simulates fucking her with the device but she's exhausted and numb and no longer aroused. He slides the wet vibrator up to her anus and pushes slightly but settles for just rubbing the wetness around the rim.

"Pleasure and pain, Prisoner 5872. Just a taste of each."

He walks to the door and unlocking and opening it tells his secretary to come in and see to the prisoner. He leaves the door wide open so the guard is able to look in and get an eyeful.

The Warden returns to his desk and signs the early release form with a flourish. Without even glancing over at the bed he leaves the room without a word.

The secretary quickly unbuckles the four restraining straps and helps Prisoner 5872 to sit up and put her uniform back on. Every part of the inmate, from her waist to her knees, is suffering from burning, stabbing pains and even just sitting on the bed is torture. She shivers in fear over what a real punishment would entail.

Prisoner 5872 stands with difficulty and falters after a step but the guard has come into the room now to help the secretary move her out.

"My release form!" she cries, gesturing to the desk. Her entire ordeal was endured to achieve this precious bit of signed paper. The secretary brings it into the reception area where the FAX machine is.

"I'm sending it right now," she demonstrates, stating: "You'll be leaving tomorrow." Glancing down at the document she looks into the tear-streaked face of the humbled woman being held upright by the guard and adds: "Cheryl."

The End

The Honeymoon is Over

"Uh-oh, look's like the honeymoon's ended for those two," remarks a gossipy old uncle at the family party. An equally elderly woman follows the direction of his gaze and cackles a laugh.

"That's my great-niece, I was at their wedding. A pretty virgin with that big strapping man glued to her side, crazy about her he is."

"Crazy with jealousy right now," the old man states. The two of them watch the husband tightly holding the waist of his much-younger bride who stumbles to keep up with him as they hurry across the lawn to the road. Angry tension shows in the stiffness of his gait.

Her embarrassed cries are faint but still audible to the avid listeners who elbow each other in gleeful appreciation of the show.

"He's in a raging temper!"

"Yup, caught by the green-eyed monster."

One car slips out of the line of limos and the chauffeur has the back door open by time the Don arrives. Furious, he bodily throws his young wife into the back-seat and following her inside slams the door before Enrico has a chance to close it. The driver hurries around to get behind the wheel and head out.

The wizened old relatives smile as their minds stretch back over the years to times of youthful passion and sexual excitement.

"The deflowered bride has discovered the power she holds between her legs," the old woman states before looking around and asking: "Who was she flirting with? Do you know?"

"No, but I bet it's that guy over by the food tent who's nursing a bleeding nose. It's probably broken and considering what I've heard about Don Vincenzo he got off lightly."

"But he can't blame him, not really, because young men will always follow when a pretty girl leads. I bet she's the one who's going to be taught a lesson she won't soon forget!"

They share knowing grins as the old man comments: "The handsy young man will ache all night from that face punch but that naughty young wife won't sit comfortably all week!"

The subjects of this speculation, Don Vincenzo and his new wife Lenora, are having a heated exchange in the limo. He's accusing her of flagrant, slutty behavior and she's yelling right back that he's an overbearing and over-reacting jealous man with his mind in the gutter.

"You are mine!" he roars, adding: "This body of yours belongs to me and only me. I will be the only man who ever touches you or is touched by you. You should know this already, in fact I know you do know, but you're testing me. I've been far too soft, but that ends now!"

Pinching her chin between his strong fingers the Don forces his wife to meet his eyes as he continues his rant, threatening: "You're going to learn that I will not hesitate to punish you, harshly and immediately, whenever I decide you need it and no matter where we are."

Despite Lenora's protests the Don flips her over his knee but before he pulls up the skirt of her summer dress he says to his driver:

"Enrico, we've got a twenty minute trip to get home and I'm going to spend every minute of it spanking my errant wife. When we arrive don't open the door till I knock on the partition. Now close it up quickly because my palm is itching to get to bare this naughty girl's bottom and get to work."

Lenora pleads for mercy while Enrico grins to himself thinking of the licking his boss's new wife is about to get. He hopes she can learn to enjoy it because the Don certainly will. It will be to everyone's benefit if he can access a plump bottom to target his moods on. Surely the girl sensed she was getting a stern disciplinarian for a husband? Maybe not though, it was an arranged marriage after all. Well, at least the boss will be in excellent spirits when he's done.

Lenora has heard stories about her husband's fabled temper. People fear him saying he's quick to use his fists - *and more* – so it's best to stay on the Don's good side. Her own mother warned her to be an obedient, docile wife.

She believes the rumors but knows that *her* Vin won't hurt her. He's crazy about her body, he just loves it and her. On their wedding night he was so tender and gentle taking her virginity. He was rough with passion the next morning but then spent ages kissing and caressing the faint bruises he'd left behind.

She knows he will never truly harm her, but he won't equate a spanking with abuse, just old-fashioned discipline that he thinks she deserves. Recalling spankings she received when her younger self got into trouble makes her shudder at the thought of what her husband might do.

"You can't spank me, I'm not a child—"

"That's right you're not, so you're going to be given a misbehaving wife's spanking, not a child's light paddling. You're getting a painful punishment that your ass will remember for days."

He begins by pulling the hem of her dress up to her waist and her panties down to her knees. Ever since their wedding night he's enjoyed playing with Lenora's body, worshipping her breasts, bottom, and vagina, but now she needs some firm manhandling. Now he needs to think about her tits, ass, and cunt.

The spanking begins with smacks moving up and down from one cheek to the other but soon settles into a steady rhythm of several strokes here, then there, then there.

"When I saw you naked for the first time your ass was so luscious I hoped you'd be a sassy wife I could discipline. Your pretty derriere is designed for the *good girl spankings* a bratty girl invites to please herself and her husband."

Vin concentrates most of his swats on the fleshiest part of her delectable bottom but makes sure to give extra stinging slaps to her sit spots and thighs. Soon that whole area of his wife's body is inflamed and the deep pink color brings a satisfied smirk to his face.

"It's a shame your first time across my knee is for a *bad girl punishment.* The kind of correction that makes a young lady feel very sore and sorry for herself."

Lenora huffs and flinches, resolutely refusing to cry, but as the spanking continues she can't help but squirm and wiggle in a futile attempt to evade his hard palm. Vin holds her in place while his hand keeps delivering one sharp slap after another. He alters the weight of his strokes to create a variety of smacking sounds.

Soon his woeful bride is loudly crying and moaning: "Please Vin, please... no more, I beg you. Please stop, I promise I've learned my lesson."

"Oh I'm not even close to being done with you, wife. I've turned your ass a pretty shade of pink but it will be a blistering red before I'm done."

She pleads for mercy and promises to never, ever even glance at another man but that only makes him chuckle as he agrees that *no, she won't.*

In a burst of anger Lenora swears and yells but that only makes Vin hit even harder.

Her hips buck in a frenzy, desperate to escape the stinging pain, but he won't relent. Lenora doesn't realize how much pleasure Vin gets from exerting control in this manner. Her sobs only encourage him to take her further into the pain. He will make her bow to his will and he'll enjoy his dominance with every stroke administered.

"Only a defiantly wayward wife would smile at another man while he strokes her hair. In public, too!"

That memory drives Vin to unleash a flurry of extra-hard spanks that sets Lenora's limbs kicking out. He uses his right leg to trap hers in place and she's reminded of just how vulnerable she is. Her tender flesh is at the mercy of her dominant and domineering husband and he's exacting a cruel torment.

After what feels like an eternity to Lenora's burning bum Vin stops but only long enough to pull her tits free from the low-cut bodice of her sundress. He'd noticed men, especially that jerk he'd had to deck, staring at her cleavage. This position across his lap with her arms held behind her back forces Lenora's fresh young breasts to jut out.

That's some view, he thinks, admiring her tits. *In fact, this is a hell of a sight with her half-naked squirming while pinned across my knee.* She squeaks in surprise when he rubs his hot palm across her hard little nipples.

"You feel how much heat has transferred from your ass to my hand? Well, I'm not done yet, wife," and with that pronouncement the hard paddling resumes. He watches her tits bounce every time his hand connects with her ass.

Lenora shrieks and wails as the hot pain intensifies with each new swat. She can't understand how Vin can do this to her. *Doesn't he love me anymore? Is my body no longer the precious gift he claimed it to be?* Her tears signify the end of something she had and she feels the loss with regret. She really did enjoy the power her pussy held over him so much but now...

After this things will never be the same between us, she thinks. I will always know that he is able to do this to me whenever he likes and for however long he wants. What if I spill his coffee or laugh at the wrong thing - will that be enough for him to flip me over and bare me for another spanking without a second thought? This changes everything.

Leonora feels so sorry for herself now and for all the future spankings she'll receive. It never occurs to her to simply behave herself.

When his bride's sobs dwindle to a snuffling crying and her shoulders flop down in limp resignation Vin knows the lesson has been delivered. His wife will think twice before shamelessly flirting again.

Roughly massaging the bright red flesh he's already anticipating the next opportunity to discipline Lenora. He can't wait to introduce her to the sexy foreplay spankings he's sure will turn her on but personally? he prefers punishment.

The car has been at a standstill for some time now, Vin knows Enrico will have delivered them to the front door. He knocks on the privacy glass and when it slides down instructs Enrico to drive them into the underground garage *then come around and open the back-door on the driver's side.*

Lenora struggles to cover up but her husband holds her firmly in place, leaving her breasts and bottom exposed despite her begging protests. When Enrico opens the correct door he holds his head stiffly in order to only look into his boss's eyes.

Vin nods in appreciation at his employee's tact then hands over his phone and says: "I want you to take some photos of my wife's tear-stained face, and if I lift my right leg up like this can you get her punished ass in the shot, too?"

Enrico sights through the camera's lens and nods. He takes several photos while Vin admonishes Lenora to look up at the camera. Filled with shame she does as she's told. Then the Don orders his driver to come around to the other door so he can get some shots from a new angle.

Vin nudges Lenora's thighs apart wanting the camera to capture the slickness of her slit and the extreme redness of her well-spanked bottom. Her embarrassment is paralyzing as he warns Enrico to forget what he's seeing and to never discuss it.

"And make sure I'm in the picture too," says Vin, resting his hand on her punished thigh and highlighting his size against hers. After several more photos are taken Enrico hands back the phone and the Don tidies his wife's clothes.

"I won't make you wear these right now," he says pulling her panties over her feet before dropping her skirt down.

Pocketing them he adds: "Actually, I'm going to start a collection of the panties you were wearing ahead of a spanking. On those occasions when I warn you hours in advance that you've earned a trip across my knee I bet I'll have to peel the panties from this wet little cunt," he says giving her swollen clit a pat.

Leonora staggers when Vin lifts her off his lap so he steps out of the car scooping her over his shoulder as he stands up.

"Oh please Vin, put me down and let me walk! I don't want anyone to see me this way—"

"No!" he snaps cutting her off. "You can count yourself blessed that Enrico will spread the word that the Don has his wife well in hand. Be properly submissive now and I won't parade your red naked butt for everyone to see. I'm sure the staff would applaud my dominance over their wilful mistress."

"Please don't do that, Vincenzo. Please, please!"

"I won't this time sweetheart, but never push your luck." He lays a proprietary hand on her rear, but gently. "You've been properly punished, Lenora, and now I'm gonna fuck you from behind so I can admire my handiwork."

To her humiliation and his delight Lenora's spanking has her dripping wet and ready for her husband's cock. Setting her on her hands and knees he strokes her clit until she loudly screams through an orgasm.

He gets hard watching how her red ass jiggles so he keeps stroking until she's crying out in ecstasy again and then he pounds in to her. She clenches around him every time his groin slaps against her throbbing bottom and he climaxes with a roar.

The entire household hears the master taking his pleasure and they are very pleased at the happiness he'd found with his flighty young wife.

When two of the photos Enrico took are enlarged, framed, and hung on one wall of Vin's walk-in closet the upstairs maid sneaks staff in to have a good look and a giggle.

Despite his wife's pouting Vin refuses to take the pictures down so Lenora has to pretend she doesn't know what the servants are doing every time they put his clean clothes away. Sometime the photos inspire him to take action so she's always half-anxious, half-hopeful if he lingers in there for an extra long time.

Whenever he has to spend time away from his bride Don Vincenzo lustily strokes himself to completion while studying a particular photo on his phone: a close-up shot of Lenora biting her lip with a beseeching look on her beautiful tear-streaked face.

The End

Also by Lucy Lafferty

She's Just Bad
She's Gonna Get It Now!
She's Getting It Again!

Standalone
Santa's Christmas Party with the Littles: a DD/lg Age Play and Age Gap
Short Story
A New Year's Resolution for Boss Daddy's Tardy Middle
A Valentine's Day Punishment for a Naughty Middle's Vandalism
Doll Learns a Different Lesson at the St Patrick's Day Masquerade
Dared to Bare
Easter Eggs For Sylvie
Tammy's April Fool's Prank
Celebrating the Fourth of July at Bandits BDSM Club
The Bandits BDSM Club Collection

Watch for more at https://lori-laidlaw-novelist-bvwonn.mailerpage.io/
projects-copy.

About the Author

Lucy writes teasing stories of dominant men giving their brats well-deserved OTK spankings. *Then the sexy fun begins!*

Read more at https://lori-laidlaw-novelist-bvwonn.mailerpage.io/projects-copy.

www.ingramcontent.com/pod-product-compliance
Lightning Source LLC
Chambersburg PA
CBHW020330130626
46549CB00003B/1102